BLURB

Bearfoot @ Xmas was originally release as part of a Christmas Anthology (Santa's Naughty List) to raise money for Saint Jude Children's Hospital. It was only available for the 2015 Christmas Season. However it is now available to read as a stand alone.

"Lexi Cavanagh is a special investigator for the Parks and Wildlife Rangers Service. When she tracks a group of illegal poachers into Duke Greysons territory will he (A Bear Shifter) accept a human as a mate?"

BEARFOOT @ XMAS

A PARANORMAL SHIFTER ROMANCE

MELISSA BELL

ACKNOWLEDGMENTS

Jordin Thiele
Editor/Content Enhancer

EMGARRY
Editor/Proofreader

Best Wishes to You All
For
A Very Merry Christmas
And
A Safe and Prosperous
New Year!

CHAPTER 1

It was four days till Christmas. Lexi Cavanagh had been tracking a particular syndicate of wildlife poachers for nearly four months now. She'd already relocated three times during the course of her investigations, as they seemed to be working their way up the east coast. She no longer knew what it felt like to set down roots or to call a place home. She'd gone from being the epitome of an army brat to a decorated police officer, and now she was a special consultant for the Park Rangers Service. She yawned as she drove up to the front door of her latest temporary housing. Following the pattern along the coastline, she hoped that she'd finally catch a break in the case and get ahead of the trappers before they made it into bear country. She had a soft spot for the big furry guys. She thought of it a lot like the ocean; if you don't want to be eaten by a big shark, then stay the fuck out of the water, or find a damn swimming pool. Same for the wilderness; if you don't want to be eaten by a bear, then stay the fuck out of their habitat, simple.

There was already a light dusting of snow on the ground, and her boots crunched as she neared the back of her SUV. She grabbed her jacket and travel bag, then out of habit she locked her vehicle, laughing at herself. Who the fuck in their right mind would be out in this neck of the woods to take her ride? Especially parked right outside the ranger's cabin. She rolled her eyes at her big city girl style, then glanced around quickly to see if anyone had noticed, before shaking her head at herself in amusement.

As she neared the front door, she stomped her feet to shake lose any flakes of snow that had attached themselves to her boots. She entered the cabin expecting to find a front counter and an office of some sort, but instead she felt as though she'd walked straight into a scene from the 18th century. All the curtains were closed, and it was considerably dark inside the cabin. There didn't seem to be any lights left on even though the rangers had been notified of her arrival. Lexi figured that being this far from civilisation, there was a high likelihood that she'd have to look for a generator of some sort, to power things up while she was there.

Deciding to wait until daylight, she headed instead for the fireplace and lit a fire. At the same time, she wondered where the occupants of the colonial dwelling were. She'd read in the file from headquarters that this particular wildlife sanctuary was taken care of by two brothers, Duke Greyson and his brother Brent. She curled up in front of the fire with a blanket and within minutes she'd fallen asleep.

~

Duke Greyson was heading back to base after another long day of searching for his brother. They'd had an argument the day before about how boring and unfulfilling their lives had become. Brent had told Duke that he needed to lighten up a little, and in no uncertain terms, he should pull his bad attitude out of his ass where it had been hibernating for far too long and go to town. At least if he got laid it might take the rough edges off his personality and smooth out the cranky crinkles.

At six feet, four inches tall he had to duck to avoid hitting his head on a low-hanging branch. When he rose back to his full height, he could smell the aroma of burning timber. He knew that it was too damp in this part of the woods for a forest fire, so he presumed someone had lit a fire back at the cabin. He sent up a silent thank you, thinking it was his missing brother. It wasn't anything new for them to argue or even fight in bear form, but usually Duke would call a truce and storm off by himself somewhere until his temper cooled down. This time however, it had been Brent who had stormed off to calm down. Duke expected him back long before now and was beginning worry he may have run into some kind of trouble.

He knocked the sediment off his boots against the bottom step, then removed them at the back door before entering the cabin. The sweet scent of apples and cinnamon invaded his brain and his nostrils flared. The bear inside his head growled from deep inside his chest… Mine.

His feet were moving in the direction of the mouth-watering aroma before he could regain control over his own actions. He came to a halt and tilted his head at what he discovered to be the source of his bear's agitation.

She was beautiful, stunning… 'Mine,' his bear growled again, as he ran out of adjectives to describe the female sitting in his chair. He smirked to himself as he remembered the tale of 'Goldie Locks and The Three Bears' his mother used to tell them when they were only little. His cock stirred to life, quickly hardening behind the zipper of his jeans, reminding him it had been way too long since he'd been into town. Maybe his brother had been right; his bear growled savagely at the thought of being with any other woman except the one sleeping in front of him.

When she shuffled in the chair and moaned in her sleep, he almost lost it. His bear clawed its way to the surface to get a better look at their mate.

He vaguely recalled his brother saying something about an investigator who was headed this way, but with the room so full of her delicious fragrance, he couldn't concentrate, not even if his life depended on it.

L exi was dreaming of a man; she was laid out like a smorgasbord in front of a raging fire. Her hand sank into his dark brown hair as his mouth covered her hot, wet pussy. She could feel the heat of the flames warming her bare skin as she arched her back to offer her clit to the flicks of his eager tongue. She moaned in appreciation of his oral skills as he lavished her lady bits with a graze of his teeth, making her juices flow. She squirmed to gain a closer connection, to direct his attention, but he held her in place with his strong forearms and hands which were the size of a giant bear's. She widened her legs around his broad shoulders as he fucked her with his tongue. Languidly, he lapped up her nectar as every tantalizing stroke liquefied into a gush on his lips. As her orgasm overtook her, she cried out and sat up on her elbows to see who this unbearably talented man was.

Dazed, she looked around and blushed at the knowledge that the stranger leaning against the wall studying her had witnessed her erotic dream. Her inner walls pulsed with another strong contraction and she felt her juices dampen her underwear. When she saw his eyes shimmer amber, and his nostrils flare, she whispered to herself, "Kill me now, poachers be damned."

From another location inside the small cabin, the crackled sound of a two-way radio broke the awkward moment. "Big bear, this is little bear. You got your ears on?"

Duke looked over his shoulder and down the hall, then quickly spun on his heel. "Fuck!" He knew if his brother was using the radio with that much static, he was further away than he'd hoped.

"Repeat, big bear…"

"Big bear receiving. Advise of your location."

"I'm out past Gertrude's, she reported two cubs missing. I'm gonna stay at Papa Bears' tonight and organize a search party from here. Big bear, it doesn't look good. I found tire tracks about two miles from here on my way up the range."

CHAPTER 2

Duke replaced the handset and turned to study the woman standing in the doorway. It was obvious from the clothes she was wearing and the logo on her rather ample breast that she was part of the Parks and Wildlife Rangers Services. His entire night had just gone to hell in a hand-basket, one that was made of twigs and dried mud. Before he could figure out how he was going to carry off the damn thing without a handle, the woman stepped forward with her hand out-stretched to greet him.

"Hi, I'm Lexi Cavanagh. I believe Head-quarters sent word last week to say I'd be in the area to track down some illegal trappers."

"Yeah, my brother mentioned something about it a couple of days ago. He's over the other side of the reserve at the moment. I'm Duke, Duke Greyson, and that was my brother Brent you just overheard on the radio." He captured her much smaller hand in his and watched her cheeks pinken as she blushed. His shaft throbbed as he found himself wondering what her full figure looked like without her uniform on. His thoughts went south, and they both stood there in limbo, holding hands for longer than necessary only making the situation even more awkward between them.

Duke cleared his throat, then asked, "Have you eaten?"

"No, I thought I would stop and get something on the way, but then it was as though I'd dropped off the map. I couldn't find a place to stay, so I'm hoping the spot in front of the fireplace is free. I'm happy to roll out a sleeping bag and crash there, if it's not too much trouble?"

"Well I know I'm starving. The shower is run by gas so there's plenty of hot water if you'd like to freshen up." He inwardly winced, hoping she would take the opportunity to wash some of her intoxicating scent away. "I'll go and turn the generator on to get some power happening."

Lexi yawned, "Sounds good to me, Warden."

"Lexi, just call me Duke. We're all equals around here."

Lexi gave a curt nod before going to her bag and retrieving a pair of sweatpants and a t-shirt. As she turned to head for the shower, she came up against a wall of solid muscle and squeaked, "Make some noise big guy." She swallowed hard, then added, "I'm sorry, you spooked me."

Duke gave her a crooked smile, "No, I'm sorry. My mum always said I was her light-footed little bear. I guess Brent is used to me."

"Does she not call you that anymore?" she laughed, as she looked up at the man towering over her.

His smile faded, "No, she died when I was young."

"Oh, I'm sorry..." her words trailed off as her hand rose to his cheek. It was as though she couldn't help but touch him. Her empathic side wanted to offer him comfort. When she realised what she'd done, she began to pull her hand away. A rumble broke from Duke's chest that sounded an awful lot like a growl and his hand shot up to cover hers. His nostrils flared, and he took a step closer so their bodies were brushing against one another.

Duke allowed Lexi to slip her hand free, and he watched as she scurried out of sight like a frightened little mouse. He rolled his eyes as he again caught the scent of her body and suddenly all he wanted for dinner was apple and cinnamon pancakes with ice-cream. Shaking his head, he pulled a couple of venison steaks out of the fridge and began to cook them for dinner. He tossed a handful of salad ingredients into a bowl, gave it a stir and sat it on the kitchen table. He was busy cooking for his guest while thinking over how to tackle the trouble on the other side of the reserve.

He needed to find out what the story was with Lexi Cavanagh, and they also needed to find the missing cubs before the colony of bear shifters were outed to the entire world. If that were ever to happen, he had no doubt in his mind; they would all be rounded up and used for science experiments. Even at the slightest hint of their existence, the government would wipe out the entire community just to discover the next weapons' grade fighter.

The bear growled deep inside Duke's chest as its mate entered the room, effectively pulling him from his thoughts.

He plated the steaks and sat one on the opposite side of the table from where he stood. "I hope you like medium/rare."

"Love it, only way to eat meat."

The rumble started low in his belly and resonated through the room as he chuckled. "Have a seat, help yourself to some salad. Do you want any sort of dressings or sauces?"

"No thanks, I like my salad naked," Lexi

replied, then felt her cheeks heat up, as she sat down clumsily in the offered chair. She kept her eyes down on her food as the imposing male only laughed harder and louder.

She cleared her throat. "So, you said your brother was on the other side of the reserve. Can we go there after dinner?"

Well that definitely shut him up, she thought as she cut into her meat and lifted it to her mouth. "Mmmm, this is good," she proclaimed, as she looked up to find Duke frowning, not at her exactly, but at her mouth. She licked her lips thinking she must have juice from the steak on them only to watch his brow furrow harder.

Duke's eyes lifted to meet her stare when he realised she'd stopped chewing and had swallowed her mouthful. Her second bite paused midway between her plate and her open mouth. Lexi could have sworn that she'd seen a shimmer of dark amber glaze over the chocolate brown irises of Duke's eyes, but then she dismissed it as a trick of the light. Her heart sped up, and she quickly shoved the bite size chunk of meat into her mouth. When she tried to stab a cherry tomato, it leapt from her plate and landed on Duke's.

Without taking his eyes off Lexi, he picked up the stray vegetable or fruit, or whatever the hell it was, and popped it into his own mouth.

"Hey, that was mine," she giggled, piercing one hidden under some lettuce on Duke's plate and stealing it out from under his nose.

Duke really liked the way her eyes lit up when she laughed, and he was finding out the thought of taking a mate wasn't nearly as scary as he'd imagined. The only complication was that he couldn't re-member anyone of his clan ever claiming a human as a mate. It was probably best not to even think about it, at least not while she was within reach. His fingertips tin-gled to follow the features of her face, to rest on her pulse and see if he could make it race like she was doing to his own as it thundered against his ribcage. He recalled that Lexi had asked him a question, but he'd been too enthralled by her presence to respond.

"Umm, no," he finally replied.

"Sorry?" Lexi asked, thinking he was referring to the tomato exchange.

"You asked if we could head to the other side of the reserve after dinner and the answer is no."

"Oh, okay," Lexi offered awkwardly.

Duke's hand covered hers, "I don't think you understand." He explained, "It's a two-day trek across rough terrain and we'd have to check the weather before we leave. We can head out in the morning if all goes well. I'm supposed to be on that side of the mountain for Christmas, anyway. So, I guess a day or two early is neither here nor there when it comes to family."

"Wow! Really?"

"Hang on, I could see if Santa is headed in that direction and we'll hitch a lift on his slay." He grinned, and she couldn't help but enjoy the playful ribbing. The last station she'd visited she was forced to deal with an old guy who burped, farted and snored, so this was a very pleasant and enjoyable change.

"Shotgun!" Lexi laughed out loud.

After satisfying their hunger, Duke offered her a hot chocolate to drink in front of the fireplace where he thought it would be more comfortable. They sat and talked for about an hour until Lexi dozed off while Duke was asking her about the men she was tracking. He wanted to know why she wasn't at home in the arms of a loving male, or visiting with her family for the holidays, but she managed to avoid answering his questions by conveniently falling asleep.

He walked down the hall to his bedroom and pulled down the covers, then returned to lift her into his arms, and carry her to his bed.

CHAPTER 3

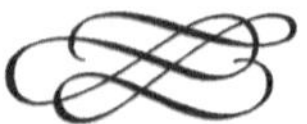

Duke rinsed out the cups then had a hot shower before turning in for the night. He'd just gotten into his brother's bed when he heard the sound of the wind outside pick up and at the same time the generator stalled from lack of fuel. In the distance, he could hear the howl of the resident wolf pack echo as they bayed at the moon. His inner bear nudged at his skin in an attempt to signal its desire to be with its female. Duke growled back inside his head to indicate that he was well aware of what the damned beast wanted, but it wasn't going to happen. Regardless of his denial, his manhood had been unbearably throbbing like a sore thumb for hours. He cursed himself for not taking care of his affliction in the shower, but unfortunately, he knew that now he'd scented his mate, he would remain hard until he claimed her. Masturbation would only make matters worse for him on a physical level and he refused to be overbearing; only feral animals did that sort of thing.

It was why the wolf pack had slowly been dying out over the past century; they'd lost their humanity and given into the beast until eventually they were cursed with only male offspring, and no females to breed with. It was also why they no longer shifted, their alpha had damned them to their beasts' bodies after his daughter was pack raped the night before a full moon.

The thought of making the journey to the other side of the reserve with Lexi made his bear uneasy, but the idea of leaving her here alone was enough to raise the hairs on the back of his neck. It was out of the question. He'd just have to take precautions, that's all. Duke knew that

Lexi being a human might be an issue for his clan, but he strongly suspected it wouldn't necessarily bother the wolf pack. Not to mention the complication of the missing bear cubs or poachers skirting the reservation. He found it damn near impossible to fall asleep. Suffocated inside his own skin, and surrounded by the scent of cinnamon apples, yet not being able to taste them from their source, was pure torture. Eventually he knew he needed to get some fresh air and his bear was clawing at him to be released. With a heavy sigh, he got out of bed and left the warmth of the cabin. On the opposite side of the timber shed, he removed his clothes and tilting his neck from left to right he cracked it to relieve some of the tension before he shifted. Taking a couple of steady breaths, he focused on slowing down his human heart rate and allowing his bear to take over. The transition was seamless, spontaneous and painless, if anything in his present state of arousal it was a minuscule relief. Until the bear took control of their shared body and insisted on rubbing his scent against every object, he could find surrounding the exterior of the house.

L exi woke up to the most amazing fragrance she'd ever smelt; it was warm and spicy and it made her feel at home. She rolled over to try to go back to sleep but the uncomfortable pressure of a full bladder prevented her from doing so. With a begrudging sigh, she climbed out of the massive bed and made her way down the hall to the toilet. She returned to the bedroom which she had concluded was Duke's, simply because of the tantalising cologne that filled the air. Lexi pulled back the curtain to check what the night's weather was like. She gasped at what she saw. A large grizzly bear was only a short distance away from her window. At first, she thought he'd simply been passing through and stopped to scratch an itch against a tall solid tree. But when it turned to glance in her direction, then repeated the same movements against the side of the cabin, Lexi recognised it for what it was doing. The bear was busy marking its territory.

She could have stood there all night watching, but the bear seemed to take too much of an interest in her standing on the other side of the glass. Not game to move in case it decided she looked like food, she stood motionless. The only visible sign that she wasn't a statue was her warm breath as it fogged up the windowpane. She held the air in her lungs as it moved in to rub up against the windowsill in front of her, then as it pushed itself up on its hind legs, the back of its skull connected harshly with the overhanging roof. Her palm settled on the glass, and she wished she could run her hands through its thick winter fur. It shook its head and bounced back down on all fours with a low growl. Its nose touched the glass on the opposite side of where her hand rested. It licked the surface and paused, almost waiting for some kind of reaction. Without warning, it turned and ambled back down onto the snow-covered ground then disappeared around the corner of the shed. Even after the bear had left her view, she stood frozen on the spot, mesmerised by the entire experience.

Duke's heart sped up to match that of his human form's regular beat as he shifted. He quickly pulled his clothes back on then took a peek at his bedroom window. He paused as he watched the expression on Lexi's face. She was irresistible, and he was undeniably drawn to her, but she was human. When the curtain dropped back into place, he ran across the snow-covered gap between the woodshed and the cabin.

He climbed back into bed feeling only somewhat better after stretching his legs and taking in the fresh night air. The little sleep he had, had been restless and disturbed by dreams of tasting Lexi's nectar as he stirred her body to create an everlasting flow to quench his own desire.

Eventually he gave up on the idea of sleep and began to get things packed up and ready to take his female to meet his clan.

Lexi's nose told her it was time to get up. She rubbed her eyes, still tired from her journey and a broken night's sleep. She found Duke in the kitchen with a dish towel tossed over his shoulder, getting food ready. He stilled as she entered. "You hungry?" he asked.

"Actually, I'm famished." She laughed. "I'm not usually one to eat breakfast, but then good service is hard to find. I mostly settle for instant coffee and a piece of toast."

"Well we need to make sure we have the energy to hike hard. We don't want to get stuck between here and the half-pass. We have a smaller cabin in the middle between here and where my cl... family are." He corrected himself quickly, then covered his faux pas by sliding a plate across the table.

"Wow." She looked at the size of the helping he'd shovelled onto it. She turned it one way then the other, aimlessly looking for a single area of the plate that wasn't covered by food. She looked up at him as he handed her a mug, then filled it with a strong brew. The aroma of it made her scalp tingle in anticipation.

"Do you want sugar or creamer?" he asked, before taking a seat opposite her with his own mountain of food in front of him.

Lexi watched as he packed away the entire contents of his plate. It reminded her of a body builder she'd once dated in her senior year. She smiled behind her cup at the memory. She'd only gone out with him because she knew her father didn't like him and she was desperate to prove a point. When she didn't get the reaction she'd wanted, she broke up with him.

"Any word on the missing bear cubs, have they been found?"

"No, nothing," he sighed.

Lexi reached out, her hand covered his. "We'll find them. They don't usually kill their captives as far as we can tell. The guys I'm following, they hunt, trap and sell their prey alive on the black market. To be able to afford that kind of cargo, they have to be really rich or well sponsored."

Not wanting to say too much and give away any secrets, Duke just nodded. Then added, "I hope so." After a moment's silence he offered, "I've put some long thermal underwear out for you, as well as an extra jersey. The weather report says it looks like there's a significant cold front moving in. We'll probably have a foot of fresh snow before we reach shelter." Duke was all too aware that once they left the cabin, they would have no contact with his brother until they made camp at dusk. At this time of the year, the days were very short, so they needed to make good time. He just hoped they'd hear good news from Brent to say the cubs had been found.

Kirk (*Kuruk – Pawnee for Bear*) slowly opened his eyes and looked around. His vision was still a little fuzzy, and he had a horrible taste in the back of his throat. 'Shit!' he thought. He and his brother were locked in a damn cage. Kohan (*Kohana – Sioux for Swift*) was always getting them into some sort of trouble. At twelve, he should have known better. They both should be leading by example for their younger siblings and cousins. Yet there they were locked in a cage, and if his head didn't hurt so much, he knew he'd be able to pick up on the obvious thing he'd overlooked.

He jumped as something hit the bars behind him making him growl. When he attempted to turn in that direction to see what or who was behind him, his world suddenly came crashing down around both he and his brother. He was no longer in his bear form. 'Shit! Shit! Shit!' Their secret was out. Something touched his bare upper thigh and as pain ratcheted through his body, he again became the bear.

"It's a boy," he heard a gruff male voice say, as he lay panting on the floor of the cage. His paws throbbing as though they were going to explode.

"What about the other one?" a different guy asked.

"Doesn't matter, we've got the full order as long as they all shift. We just have to wait for them to wake up." The first voice replied. "If they don't turn, then we'll kill them and find new ones."

Kirk's world turned black as a wolf snarled and gnashed its teeth at the bars behind him.

Lexi put her boots on only to have Duke rub them both with a pungent concoction. "What is that?" she asked with a wrinkled nose.

"It's to block your scent so the wolves can't smell you."

"Oh, okay." She shrugged, "Yeah, I'd

rather not be seen as a food source." She joked about her curves self-consciously. "Because this does not run," she laughed, indicating her thickness.

"I'll keep that in mind if ever I decide to chase you." He lifted his gaze to meet hers through hooded lashes to watch her blush.

CHAPTER 4

Duke had sensed the pack moving through the surrounding terrain ever since they'd first left the cabin. His attempts at covering Lexi's scent with his own had been a massive failure. They had closed in even tighter after she squatted behind a bush to pee. The excitement in their howls told Duke they were well aware that his travelling companion was indeed a female. An unmated one at that. His bear growled at him from inside his skull, chastising him for not listening to his instinct in claiming their mate before now.

Lexi noticed a change in Duke. He was

suddenly all about the business end of the stick. When she'd tried to make conversation with him by asking about the wolves, he'd put his fingers to his mouth to shush her. Every so often he would stop in front of her and listen. For what, she had no idea. The howls didn't seem to get any closer although the hairs on the back of her neck rose in warning and she knew they were being stalked. 'Great, I'm a Christmas banquet for the holiday season,' she thought, suddenly feeling like 'Little Red Riding Hood' afraid of the big bad wolf.

Not watching where she was putting her feet, she almost face planted into the snow. Duke caught her before she landed, and as she opened her mouth to thank him, his lips collided with hers on a growl. His tongue speared in between her chilled lips, heating her body all the way to her core. The man could seriously lip-lock. As her curves moulded into his hard planes, she could feel an unfamiliar fire in her belly. It broke into two halves, one rising to resonate in her chest, melting her heart, the other moving lower towards her uterus, making her want to surrender herself in the most wicked of ways. Sadly, it was all over before it began and Duke broke the connection with another low growl in the back of his throat.

"Sorry, I shouldn't have done that," he offered.

"Umm, yeah," Lexi replied softly, the disappointment evident on her face as well as in her tone.

Duke wanted to hit something. She wasn't supposed to be his mate, she was human. One hundred percent, bona-fide, without a shadow of doubt, fucking human. He needed to get to the other side of the reserve and quickly. At least there, he could ask the clan's spiritual healer to heal the aching heart of his bear.

When he spun around to resume his path, he found it was blocked by three savage wolves, all with their heads low and their teeth exposed in a snarl. With a cursory glance to his left and right, he confirmed his suspicions, they were completely surrounded on all sides.

"Give us the girl and we'll leave. There's no need for bloodshed," Lexi heard a male's voice demand from somewhere close by.

"Delsin, you cannot have what is not yours," Duke growled.

Lexi took a step closer to Duke, turning slowly to find there was a wolf covering any and all possible escape routes.

"Well I beg to differ. I do not see your claim," he arrogantly stated.

"Duke?" Lexi cried as the wolf nearest to her took a step closer. She lifted her hand to her gun and released the clip. But before she could palm her weapon and take aim, she heard the one Duke had identified as Delsin bark an order at the surrounding pack of wolves. She screamed like a little bitch as the wolf to her right and left were suddenly transformed into men, very naked men. Their hands wrapped around her upper arms in an unbreakable hold. She was terrified. She began to wonder if she was still asleep, trapped in a nightmare. Only her cold, tired feet told her otherwise. No matter how hard she fought, she couldn't break free from the men intent on separating her from Duke.

"Let me go!" she demanded, digging her feet in to drag through the snow.

"Dude, this bitch is so loud she's hurting my ears."

"Then shut her up!" Delsin commanded with the snap of his fingers.

Duke gave into the shift the moment they tried to take his mate from him. His clothes had shredded as he suddenly became all teeth and claws unleashing an angry growl that was loud enough to vibrate the snow from the low tree branches for as far as the eye could see.

"Oh, I see now," Delsin retorted as he drew near to the female and sniffed at her ponytail. He lifted his lip in distaste. "We aren't like you Duke. We simply don't care that she's human."

Lexi had already well and truly passed the stage of panic and was well on the way to certifiable when her eyes focused on the massive frame of a very pissed off grizzly bear barely a few feet in front of her. In a split second of insanity, she curled her hands backwards and in a synchronised manoeuvre, she grabbed a piece of the male's hardware that was boldly still on display and twisted it at the same time as she squeezed. Her head flew back and connected with the one known as Delsin. The distraction was enough to align Duke for an attack on the rest of the wolf pack that was entering the clearing ready to take on the furious bear.

Lexi fell to the ground and rolled out of reach. As she did so, her head struck something hard from behind and everything became black as she succumbed to the pain exploding in her skull.

Duke lost all control as he saw his female wilt on the forest floor. His bear truly shaken by the possibility that his one and only true mate could die out here if he didn't protect her. His claws slashed giant, gaping gashes in the throats of the wolves that were stupid enough to get between him and his mate.

As he reached the two who had transformed into humans under Delsin's command, he opened his mouth and with the force of his powerful jaws, he crushed the first one's head before shaking it free from its owner. The second male made a lax attempt to change back into a wolf. Unfortunately for him, it was a mute effort. The grizzly was avenging the attack on his mate and with very little effort, the wolf lay disembowelled and bleeding out on the white snow.

When Duke turned towards his mate, he'd already started the shift. He took two steps then pulled up short. Delsin was hovering over Lexi's body in his wolf's form. Duke growled a warning, "Get away from my mate."

Delsin licked his teeth, and snarled, gnashing his jowls. Saliva dripped from his canine fangs. Duke dove low, wrestling his enemy to the ground clear of Lexi's body. With bone snapping reflexes, Duke grabbed Delsin's front legs and pulled them away from each other at a ninety-degree angle to the rest of the wolf's body effectively splitting its rib cage and rupturing the bastard's heart inside its own chest. Satisfied that the area had been cleared of any and all threat, Duke stood up and raced over to Lexi. He rolled her over to assess her injuries. She was still breathing, but she was cold enough for her lips to be tinted with a pale shade of blue. They were about an hour from the safety of the midway mark.

He quickly took stock of their belongings and grabbed a fresh set of clothes from his bag.

Duke carefully bent down and lifted Lexi into his arms before he began to leg it at double pace toward the halfway mark.

They'd reached the halfway cabin shortly before dusk just as he'd predicted. They'd never had the need for two beds in the small cabin before. When in bear form, they could make the trip in one non-stop journey. It was really only set up so that if they needed some solitude, they had a place to go to. He laid Lexi on the bed then set about starting a fire to warm her up. He lit oil lanterns and set a pot of snow over the fire to heat. He snatched up a piece of the shirt that he'd torn into shreds, when he'd shifted and dipped it into the warm water and used it to gently wipe Lexi's face. He checked her hairline at the back of her skull to find a small gash. He knew he had to wake her up. It was possible she had a concussion and he'd already had enough of a scare to last him a lifetime. He cupped her cheek and ran his thumb over her rosy lips.

"Lexi, can you hear me? I need you to wake up." He waited, stroking her stray hairs away from her face. "Come on Lexi, you need to open your eyes for me."

Lexi could hear a man's growly voice calling her. It was as though she were sur-rounded by fog and she couldn't decide which direction the sound was coming from. She frowned momentarily, but that only made the bridge of her nose ache more.

"That's it, I know you can hear me," Duke encouraged when he saw her brow draw tight.

Lexi wondered what she'd been doing to feel this lousy. She couldn't remember drinking, but it felt as though she'd tied on a wild night and now she had the worst hangover ever. She groaned as her lashes fluttered open, then she sat up suddenly at the vivid memory of what had happened moments before she passed out.

"Shhh," Duke cooed, "You're safe." He wrapped her in a bear hug, filled with relief that she was okay. Humans were so fragile. How was he supposed to be a mated to one? It just wasn't possible.

Whenever he'd gone to town to get laid, it was always with human females. It wasn't that he had anything against fucking them or anything, or rather having them fuck him and or suck on his cock. He always insisted on them being on top. That way he could control the beast inside him. Refusing to allow him to surface, his hands never touched them in passion. He was too scared he would hurt them, leave bruises, or be too rough. He silently cursed, 'Fuck!' What were the spirits thinking?

CHAPTER 5

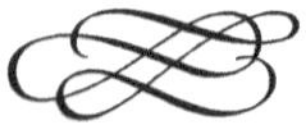

Ty (*Tyee – Chinook/Bannock meaning 'Chief'*) was the younger brother of Delsin. He was more of a loner than a part of the pack. His brother had always been threatened by his intelligence, which in his present predicament he had to question even himself. He wasn't like the rest of the feral and immoral fiends that belonged in his brother's pack. Delsin had always called him weak, but if anything, he was stronger than all of them, especially when it came to his humanity. He'd walked away in disgust, venturing to the outskirts of the forest. He knew the only way to survive the insanity of life without a mate was to go out and find her. The others all thought that staying in the sanctuary of the forest was going to keep them all safe. Physically maybe, but not so much on the mental front.

Ty snarled at the man with the fire stick, daring him to open the cage. He'd tear that fucker's throat out if only he could reach him. The third strike was enough to trigger the change, the cage becoming too small for his comfort.

"Motherfucker!" Ty cried out, before he leaned his body against the bars.

He'd put up a good fight. He would rather be put down than be someone's slave for a lousy fistful of dollars.

He watched as the kid in the cage nearest to his turn into a bear cub, and knew that if they didn't figure a way out, they were all fucked. He did a quick head-count on the men with the guns, saying a silent thank you, recognising them as tran-quilliser guns and not rifles, as he'd first thought. That probably explained the booming headache and the acrid taste in the back of his throat.

"Psst!" The kid in the cage in front of him made the sound to get his attention. He knew there was no love lost between the resident bear clan and his brother's wolf pack, but for all intents and purposes, he was no longer a part of it. He was a lone wolf, so he slid his eye in the boy's direction.

"The bald one is the leader," he whispered. "He's the one with all the keys."

Ty gave a nod to acknowledge the intel. He then lifted his head, put two fingers between his lips and whistled, "Hey Kojak!"

Lexi sat in front of the fire with a hot cup of coffee, hypnotised by the flicker of the flames as they kissed the timber, caressing it lovingly. She heard the words of the wolf-man Delsin, playing over and over in her mind. Finally, she drummed up the courage to ask, and with an apprehensive sigh she spoke, "So I'm not crazy. Shifters are real not fairytales or myths?"

"Yes, they're very real. But you can't tell anyone what you saw, or we would all be hunted down like animals - freaks for humans to experiment on. That's why we remain hidden under the cover of tales and folklores."

"What did he mean by your mark? I don't understand. What did he want with me?"

Duke had been sitting with his back against the far wall, wanting to put some distance between them. She both fascinated and terrified him. He'd been studying her from the dancing shadows of the room, trying to figure it all out.

"Many moons ago, in the times of my great ancestors, we were free to walk side by side with our spirit animals. When the white man came and settled on our lands, they killed many of the natives, so some took on the appearance of their animal spirit to escape. They were safe in animal form. It allowed them to move without detection throughout the wilderness. The animals have always instantly recognised their soul mates, but in the past several years, the wolf pack numbers have dwindled and only the males remain. They don't care who the woman is…" his words broke off at the memory of the tragic tale of Honi (*Honiahaka* – *'Little Wolf'* – *Cheyenne*). Mai (*Maiyun* – *'Wolf'* – *Cheyenne*), Honi's mother and mate to Delsin, found her daughter's battered and bruised body. Mai pointed the finger at every male in the pack that had taken a turn with her precious Honi. Delsin sentenced each and every one of them to sacrifice themselves to the beast or the blade. The cowards all chose to shift into their wolf form, and at her mate's command, the rest of the pack were told to kill them on sight if they were ever discovered in their human form again. One by one they had all been killed off by Delsin's insanity. Mai had run that night to the sanctuary of the bear clan and they'd helped her to disappear. "Anyway, that's what he wanted from you. He wanted to mate with you in an attempt to rebuild his pack."

He wiped his hand down his face to clear his thoughts. When he opened his eyes, Lexi was standing. She'd finished her hot drink and sat the empty cup on the coffee table. She'd dropped the blanket he'd wrapped around her onto the chair and was looking at the one and only large bed. When she looked at Duke, she was biting her lower lip nervously. Duke's cock instantly hardened, he wasn't blind after all. He could see her pebbled nipples under her shirt, attached to plump, cantaloupe-shaped heavy breasts. Before he could think better of it, he was on his feet moving towards the one thing he knew he shouldn't want... Shouldn't have, but for the life of him he couldn't think straight when she looked at him with those sad eyes. Someone had hurt her which made him mad. His hand sank into her hair, tilting her head upwards to expose the column of her neck. He leaned down and brushed his lips against it, then pleaded, "Tell me to stop?"

She trembled in his embrace, the tension on her scalp making her tingle in the most divine way. It had been so long since he'd been with a woman and the scent of this particular female, his mate, was driving his bear crazy. He nipped her neck in warning. "I won't be gentle," he urged, hoping she would refuse him, but at the same time, praying she didn't. When her strong fingers interwove with his hair and her fingernails grazed over his scalp, he growled.

Duke's teeth ached and his bear rose to just under the surface of his skin. It was hungry for its mate's touch; it was even hungrier to lay its claim to her body. His free hand slid down on the inside of her pants to cup her round cheek and he pulled her body against his.

Lexi was delirious with the sensory overload, his lips, his teeth, the hardness of his cock pressed to the soft curves of her belly. There was no way she was going to say a word to stop him. She wanted this, she needed it. He made her feel like a desirable woman.

One moment she was vertical, and the next she was horizontal, with the mattress rising to meet her body. Duke quickly stripped her bare of her clothes, then licked, kissed and sucked his way impatiently down her body. She cried out as his tongue lavishly licked her lower lips. He feasted on her like a starving man, ramping up her eagerness to be satisfied. He swirled his tongue over and around her clit in the most sinful way, building the fireball which was steadily inflaming her lust. When she buried her hand in his thick, soft hair and lifted her head to look down the length of her body, the shadows from the fireplace suddenly took her back to the images from her dream. Lexi cried out Duke's name as her grip on his hair tightened and she pressed her pussy against his parched lips even harder, riding out her orgasm. When her body finally relaxed back against the bed, spent, Duke rose over her.

He aligned his throbbing cock with her aching centre and in one earth shattering movement, he plunged deep inside of her.

Duke clenched his jaw tightly to prevent his beast from sinking its teeth into Lexi's skin, but he couldn't hold back the moan of pure unadulterated satisfaction of being buried to the hilt inside their mate. He slowly began to slide in and out of her tight body. He marvelled at her reaction to him being inside her. He was surprised when she started to softly chant dirty talk in his ear.

"Oh god yes! That's it… Yes… Fuck me, fuck me harder," she hissed.

Lexi was in every way perfect, except she was human and he could never forget that. She was right there with him though, she lifted and spread her legs wider for him. With her knees resting under his arms, she locked her ankles at the curve of his spine and as he pumped his hips to plunder her aching core, her inner muscles sucked him in deeper and deeper until he wasn't sure if they didn't share the same heartbeat.

Her contracting inner walls tightened their stranglehold on his manhood to the point of no return, milking his hot seed, which started from the knowing prickle at the base of his spine and traveled all the way to the built-up pressure in his balls. It sizzled from the base of his shaft to the throbbing tip of his cock. He felt scorched, raw and vulnerable. How was he supposed to walk away now that he'd had a taste? She was like an oasis in the desert, a mirage that could easily disappear if he took his eyes off of her for even just a split second. She was unlike any female he'd ever been with, or ever wanted to be with again. She'd fucking ruined him. His mood quickly sobered as he realised she was watching him. "Fuck!"

Up until Lexi, no-one has ever watched Duke cum, and she'd completely forgotten that he had been the man to turn into a bear. At his heightened stage of arousal, she'd felt his cock swell even more than before, and his eyes shimmered with amber. Yet the idea of being with him, of him being inside her, didn't bother her. However, by the look on his face, she could see small signs of regret. She placed her hand on his chest and shoved him. She had more important things to think about than to worry about what he thought of her.

CHAPTER 6

The uncomfortable silence was broken by a knock at the door. Brent was standing on the other side of the timber, naked. Duke scowled at him, "Wait here." He shut the door in his brother's face and pulled a spare pair of jeans from his bag. He looked at Lexi, who was already half dressed and his guilt sparked when she refused to look at him. He wanted to hit something… hard. The way he'd treated her was unforgivable. He'd been an absolute prick. He shook his head at himself then opened the door to toss the jeans at his brother. "Get dressed. We have company." He growled at Brent, then shut the door in his brother's face again. Duke knew his brother was oblivious to the fact that Lexi Cavanagh was his mate, but he didn't care. It was bad enough she'd seen naked wolf-men, there was no way he was about to explain the situation to him with Lexi around to hear about his jealousy on the subject.

When Brent entered, he could feel the tension and smell the sex inside the small cabin. He looked at Duke then glanced at Lexi, but didn't utter a word.

Lexi put her hand out and introduced herself, "Lexi Cavanagh, I'm the visiting parks and wildlife investigator. I've been assigned to track and locate a group of poachers believed to be working in the area."

Brent smiled, and regardless of his brothers oxidised glare, he took Lexi's offered hand and shook it. "Hi Lexi. I'm Brent, the good-looking one," he joked, earning him a clip across the back of the ear as he moved quickly out of Duke's reach. "Hey!"

Lexi laughed, and both men became

entranced by the sound of it. It was almost musical until she snorted, making both the men chuckle while Lexi plateaued and her giggle ground to an abrupt halt. Embarrassment flushed her cheeks making her even more attractive to both men.

"Have the missing cubs been found?" she asked, hopeful that they had avoided capture by the illegal traders.

"Yes, and no. I managed to track them. They're not far from Swanson's Road. They have the cubs and a wolf in cages. There looks to be four men."

Lexi suddenly gasped, "Oh my god! Are the cub's shifters too?"

Brent looked at Duke with raised eyebrows, "Really? I leave you alone for ten minutes and this is what happens?"

"Delsin and his pack tried to take Lexi from me, and she saw too much to simply wave a wand and make her forget," he retorted defensively.

Brent took stock of his brother's phrasing along with the knowledge that they'd been bumping and grinding not long before he'd shown up. Maybe it was just his imagination, but judging by the way Duke kept putting himself between Lexi and him, it showed all the typical signs of a territorial bear leaving him to wonder, 'What the fuck?' He was slapped back to reality when Lexi asked, "You traveled at night. Is there any reason why the both of you can't do what you do..." she waved her hand around as though creating magic. "How long would it take for us to reach them?"

"Oh, I like her," Brent smiled.

"Shut the fuck up," Duke snarled at his brother, as Lexi smiled at Brent, giving him a conspiratorial wink.

Ty watched as the bald guy turned in his direction. He'd found a stick in the snow next to his cage and now he was armed. All he needed was for that bastard to get close enough to use it.

A few feet from Ty's enclosure, one of

the other men called out, "Hey boss, the alarm just went off on number four."

"You lot go and check it out. If it isn't a skin-walker then kill it," he instructed them. "Leave it for the animals to feed on and bring me back my cage. I'll be ready to leave when you get back."

Baldy squatted down beside Ty's cage, overestimating the safety of the bars. It was one mistake that he wouldn't live long enough to talk about as Ty buried the stick into the man's jugular and snatched the keys from his belt. With a sly smile to himself, he watched as the dying man fell to the side and stained the snow blood red.

"Hey kid, what's your name?" Ty asked as he tried different keys to open the lock.

"I'm Kirk, and that's my brother, Kohan. I'm really worried about him. He hasn't woken up."

"Stay calm kid. You know you can't control the change if you get too emotional. Just give me a moment to get things sorted over here and I'll get you both out."

Kirk gave him a silent nod, wondering

if he would be true to his word and help them escape.

After only a few seconds, Ty threw the door to his cage open and crawled out. He quickly headed for Kirk's cage and unlocked it. The boy stood up next to him as he found the key to Kohan's tiny jail. When the other bear didn't stir, Ty issued a command to Kirk, "Stay with him. I need something to wear if I'm going to stay in this form."

He located a couple of knapsacks that were full of clothing and supplies, so he made the most of what little time they had in getting dressed. He returned to where Kohan was still unconscious and pulled him from the cage, feeling for a pulse. It was faint, but it was still there, however he wasn't all too sure of what the normal rate for a bear was anyway. It wasn't like he was a vet or anything.

"Be the bear, little man," he told Kirk. "We need to get out of here before the others come back. I need you safe so I can come back for rest of them." He snarled with distaste for the hunters. He lifted Kohan's limp body up and over his shoulder, then quickly led them away from the poacher's camp.

~

L exi walked between the two bears. They were pretty much identical in the way they looked and the way they sounded, except for when the one on her right got too close to her, the one on her left would growl in protest. And after what had happened between Duke and her earlier, she kind of liked his bear form better than his human nature, at the moment anyway. It was as though they were two halves of the same coin, but someone had used the coin for target practice and it had a big hole through the centre. Why did she always go for the ones who left her feeling raw and broken? Why couldn't she find the one who was supposed to love her, flaws and all, above all else? She just wanted a place where she could fit in and feel like she was part of the furniture.

With a low growl from Duke, they all

came to a standstill. He lifted his nose to the air, then grunted in the direction he wanted them to head. They'd only been moving on the new path for a few minutes when they heard movement in the snow just ahead of them.

Duke protectively stood on his hind legs in front of Lexi, blocking her view from the possible danger. When he dropped back down, she could see a bear cub running towards them, followed by a man carrying a second one. The male identified himself as Ty, formerly of Delsin's pack. Ty then went on to explain everything that had happened to them, then quickly shifted back into his wolf, leaving the cubs with Duke and Lexi. He was determined to rescue the freshly captured animal. Brent went with him to assist in the liberation of a fellow shifter and to catch the remaining poachers in the act. They needed to make sure nobody would ever find the bodies of the illegal trappers. They would have to make everything just vanish and disappear as though it had never happened. They would have to take care of the vehicles later.

~

They traveled the rest of the distance to where Duke's clan lived. Several of the elders were sitting around a fire keeping an all-night vigil for the lost cubs.

"I know this may sound like a stupid question, but how come you guys don't have snowmobiles?"

"We do, they are here with the Addison (Aditsan – 'Listener' - Navajo)," Duke explained.

Lexi wearily shook her head in disbelief. In the centre of the surrounding cabins there was a massive tree covered with handmade decorations. It held hand-carved animals and leather fringing Lexi had never seen anything like before. It was beautiful and the importance of the moment weighed heavy inside her chest. When Kohan was comfortable in his mother's lap, he began to stir in front of the fire. Kirk curled up beside them and fell asleep within seconds. Eden smiled at Lexi and mouthed a thank you. Don, Eden's mate, stepped closer and shook Duke's hand. Duke, in his human form was using Lexi as a shield for his nudity.

"Thanks Duke. I came home as soon as I got word. But I only arrived about an hour ago," Don assured him.

Duke slapped the back of his shoulder, "It's all good man. Everything's turned out okay, thanks to the spirits."

"Well… Umm… we should all probably try to get some sleep. We have a big day ahead of us tomorrow, being Christmas Eve." The elders of the bear clan sitting around the fire growled at Duke's reminder.

Keeping Lexi in front of him, he guided her past the small gathering and towards a cabin on the right. As he cleared the group, Lexi laughed at all the wolf whistles knowing that it was for the glorious view of Duke Greyson's ass. She smiled at the idea of having a family like that one day. They entered the small cabin and Duke switched on the lights. When Lexi looked at him with a surprised glance, he shrugged his shoulder and said, "What? It's 2015. We do have power."

"Yeah and you're the one who keeps your snow rides in someone else's garage. Need I say more?"

CHAPTER 7

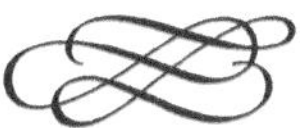

"This is nice," Lexi thought out loud, to break the silence in the room. Looking around however, she discovered it only had one bed. She shivered, "I could do with a hot shower, and some sleep."

"Lexi?" Duke said her name not really sure of what else to say.

"Don't," she replied, lifting her hand not wanting to hear, not wanting to hurt.

Words were, after all, the sharpest weapon.

"I don't need a song and dance about what happened. I'd rather just forget it ever did." She glanced away, not willing to allow him the privilege of knowing he'd hurt her.

"Lexi, it's complicated," he began. "We… shifters aren't like humans. The spirits only send us one life mate."

"Oh, I get it now." She was beginning to understand. "How could I be so stupid?" she asked herself, slapping her palm to her forehead. "I was just a little something, something." She tilted her hand up and down, and side to side to add emphases to her point. "To fill in the time till you find her, is that it?"

Duke growled in frustration with the words on Lexi's lips. All he wanted to do was kiss away her arguments.

"I don't understand what's going on either." He confessed, "I…" his loss for words pulled him up short and he drew a mental blank, as everything he had said only seemed to be making things worse between them.

"I'm not sure I believe you," she skeptically replied. "It just sounds like a piss poor excuse to me. I get it okay? I was nothing more than a way for you to scratch an itch out here in the middle of butt fuck nowhere." She glared at him.

"Shifters don't interbreed." It was a simple statement which followed through with a heavy blow to Lexi's heart. It was as though someone had let all the air out of her balloon with a little prick of unfettered words.

"Wow, who would have thought shifters could be so racist? It shouldn't matter who the person is, if their soul calls to yours, then that's all that matters," she argued.

"Did you just call me racist, just because of what I believe?"

Lexi fronted him with the lift of her chin, "If the fur fits, asshole."

"It's not the same in the shifter world as it is with humans." He scowled. "In the human world, all it takes is a fertile male and female; they have the ability to breed inter-racially. Shifters don't have that luxury, it's why we're dying out. If two bear shifters mate, they will have cubs that will all be able to transform. If two wolves mate, they will only produce shifters. But there is only a fifty percent chance that a bear and a wolf shifter could mate and produce offspring, and only twenty-five percent of them will have the ability to change. To breed with a non-shifter, that percentage lowers the ratio to only twenty-five percent, which means there is only about a ten percent chance of any possible offspring being able to shift. Do you know what that would be like for the shifter parent?"

"Oh my god, do you actually hear yourself? Are you really that stupid?" Lexi spun on her heels and stormed out, bumping into another man the size of a bear. She wiped away her angry tears of pain, bending down to retrieve her boots, not looking to see who it was.

Lexi dropped her boots back down at the door, then with a shove of her hip, she re-entered the cabin, "I'm the guest. You need to leave, not me. Go and find a cave somewhere and leave me the fuck alone." She knew she was being a bitch, but she wasn't the one who had made all the moves. Granted she wasn't innocent, she could have said no. She should have, but a fraction of vulnerability meant she'd been too weak-willed to say anything to oppose his advances. She'd obviously misread the signs because that last curve in the road was a doozy.

Ty handed Brent the keys to all the cages while he transformed into his wolf. Brent quickly hid the body of the bald-headed bastard and Ty went back inside the same cage he'd been held in before. Brent, in bear form, watched from behind a dense area of trees as the new cage was carried into the clearing. They carefully sat it down and looked around to see where their leader had gone. Their eyes suddenly leveled on the two empty bear cages.

"Where the fuck is he?" Stevenson asked.

"How the fuck should I know? I was with you dickhead," Smith replied sarcastically.

The third guy looked at the wolf. "I bet he knows," he picked up the Taser and moved toward the cage. The roar of a bear nearby gave Ty the opportunity he needed to attack. Ty's paw swung the cage door open wide, and he leapt out, his jaw latched onto the asshole's wrist making him drop the fire stick.

Brent stomped forward on his hind legs, knowing that he presented as more ferocious in that manner. The bear and the wolf worked well together as judge, jury and executioners. They both stood in front of the cage. Brent's bear growled inside his head, 'Mine' and he allowed the territorial sound to echo from his chest. At the same time, Ty's wolf snarled from deep within, 'Mine,' and he lifted his head to howl. The she-cat inside the cage hissed as she woke up abruptly and glared from Ty to Brent.

Ty and Brent both jostled with the lock to free their mate, not sure what the fuck was going on, but most of all, they were unsure of exactly what she was.

"I don't understand what she is doing here." Brent frowned, not really caring how she'd come to be in his terrain, only glad that he'd finally found his mate.

"She's not native to the area, I doubt she's even American. I've never seen anything like her before." Ty replied. "I think she's stunning," he added, offering his hand to the large cat in the cage, all too prepared for her to swipe at it. Her nose lifted and her nostrils flared, a small mewl escaped her throat, and she bumped her head against his hand. She cautiously moved out of the enclosure on wobbly legs and rubbed against Brent's side then collapsed in the snow.

"You know she's my mate?" Brent sighed, suspecting he wasn't the only one affected by the beauty of the female between them.

"You know she's mine too?" Ty established. "Is this going to be a problem?" he asked, stroking the softer than silk fur of the she-cat.

"I don't have an issue with it, unless she does. For now, as her mates, we need to get her to some place safe. I have a cabin at the edge of the reserve," Brent offered. "Did you have any plans for Christmas?"

"No. I was planning on leaving the reserve in search of my mate, but it would seem she found me instead." He stood and lifted the unconscious she-cat into his arms. "I'll carry her, you shift into the bear. You're bigger and stronger than me so you will be able to protect her better as the bear."

Brent gave a nod and allowed the change to overcome him before he led them back to the warmth of his home.

~

Duke left the cabin under protest and sought out the wise elder who always knew the answers before the questions had ever been asked. Maybe if Duke could get some clarity on the subject, then his brain and his heart wouldn't be at such odds.

Addison sat in front of the fireplace. The door was open as though he had been waiting for the young bear to seek him out. Duke lightly knocked and Addison waved him inside. The listener was always aware of what was going on when it came to his clan, yet Duke never knew how.

"Young bear, what troubles you?" Addison asked, taking a puff on his pipe.

"That depends, old man. Is that wacky weed you're smoking?"

Addison gave a sly smile and lifted an eyebrow. "Maybe it is, and maybe it isn't," he stated playfully. "Come, have a seat by my fire and talk to the listener."

Duke grumbled under his breath as he sat down. It was always the same with Addison. He listened to what you said and by the end of the one-sided conversation, you had pretty much worked out the answer for yourself. He rubbed his hands along his jeans making the comparison of talking to Addison to that of a conversation with a brick wall.

"Lexi's my mate. The bear identifies her as its female. It's just... I know I'm being a jerk, but I really had hoped to have cubs one day. She's human..." he rambled on with the pros and cons of being with a human for what felt like forever. The entire time, his mind and heart were distracted with images of Lexi's full kissable lips, the curve of her hips and the way she came apart underneath him. Finally, he stood and stormed out the door.

Addison whistled, then waved his hand at the open door. Duke turned and pulled it closed behind him, shaking his head.

"Good talking to you, young bear. See you in the morning for Christmas Eve."

CHAPTER 8

Brent shifted at the door to his cabin, then opened it for his mate and the wolf. Ty carried the white and black spotted she-cat in and gently laid her down on the bed.

"I have to let my brother know we've taken care of the situation out there. I should probably tell him that we've found my mate… I'm sorry, I meant, our mate," he explained pulling on a pair of jeans and a shirt. "I'll only be a couple of minutes. His cabin is just next door. Howl if she wakes up while I'm gone. I'd like to be here when she shifts."

Ty gave a nod "Are you sure you're

okay with all of this? I mean… me?"

Brent looked at the unconscious feline on his bed, then back at the other half of his mate-ship. "If it means I get to live the rest of my life happily providing what my mate wants and needs and if you're part of that equation, then, yeah I'm okay with it… You?"

"I think it may take some time to work out the details of the arrangement, but, I think we can make it work, for the sake of our mate. So no, I don't have a problem with it." Ty glanced at their still sleeping mate, "Let's just hope she doesn't when she wakes up and finds out what the situation is."

Brent gave a sigh. "I'll be as quick as I can," he stated as he walked out the door and headed for Duke's cabin.

He knocked and waited for a moment. At first there was no answer. So, he gave a second, slightly more impatient bang on the door.

"He's not here," Lexi informed him, her tone placid when she opened it. "Would you take me back to my truck so I can leave? I need to let headquarters know that the trail has gone cold and that I must have been mistaken. The poachers have gone elsewhere."

"What's my daft brother done now?" Brent inquired, scenting her sadness and more. "Lexi, not all of us think like my brother." He paused before opening up about what he already suspected. "A mate is supposed to be cherished and any babies or cubs born of that mating are treasures. Sometimes it seems to all come down to a man's ego, and sadly, its more fragile than the most expensive, well-crafted crystal. Give him a chance. If you still feel the same in the morning after you've slept on it, then yes, I'll return you to the ranger's station."

"Okay," she conceded due to the lateness of the hour.

"Come here." He pulled her into a hug and wrapped his arms gently around her. He lifted an eyebrow, then curiously sniffed her neck. He was right. His brother was a fucking idiot. No sooner had the thought entered his head, did the sound of his brothers pissed off growl come from behind them. He disengaged from his brother's mate and took a step away.

"I just came to tell you that the wolf and I cleaned up the problem." He looked down at the ground, then pulling his shoulders back, he lifted his head and stared at his brother. As he was about to give his brother a piece of his mind, he heard Ty's howl echo through the night. "Take care of your mate asshole," he growled as he ran past Duke, bumping shoulders with him in a silent gesture that told him they weren't done.

Lexi turned and walked the couple of steps back inside and was about to close the door when Duke's hand met with the timber. "Can we talk?"

"You know what, I'm tired." Lexi sighed. "Do we really need to do this now?"

"Please?" he begged, not wanting to wait until morning to resolve their problems… his issues. He heard Lexi's stomach growl, and he was spontaneously reminded that a good mate would've taken care of his female by hunting and caring for her needs. "Will you let me take care of you? You're hungry, and tired, and I'm… I've… never done this before." He looked away for moment before adding to his confession. "I've never wanted to do this before, so I'm going to make mistakes and I'll fuck up sometimes, but if you'll give me a chance… I do learn from my mistakes." He solemnly swore, meeting Lexi's questioning gaze.

The sincere expression on Duke's face dissolved the remaining anger which Lexi was holding onto. Maybe Brent was right. Was Duke worth giving a second chance? She gave a slight nod of her head and stepped back from the open door. As quick as lightning, Duke was inside the cabin, shutting and locking the door behind him. He walked to the dresser in the corner of the room and retrieved one of his shirts. Passing it to Lexi he told her to go and have a hot shower while he stoked the fire and prepared a late supper for them. Lexi did what he instructed, too weary to argue any further on the subject, wishing that she could hibernate for the winter and skip right past Christmas and New Year's. She wanted to wake up some place warm and sunny. The emotional toll had taken away her love for snow, and the lack of family or home had removed all of her Christmas spirit. It would be nothing more than just another day to her. She closed the bathroom door behind her and turned on the shower. She stepped in and allowed the water to wash away her humbug thoughts with its soothing heat.

B rent burst through the front door to his cabin, eager to be there for his mate when she woke. His heart raced as the she-cat hissed at both him and the wolf, making him pull up short.

"Okay. This wasn't what I expected."

The she-cat chuffed at them, uncertain of her surroundings. She leapt from the bed and raced into the bathroom. Once inside, she gave a warning growl to tell them to stay away.

"Yeah, me either," Ty agreed, looking at Brent.

Within a minute, a fair-skinned Asian female walked out, wrapped in a towel.

"Where am I?"

For a few seconds, neither man could speak, both stunned by her beauty. The small black patterned markings which traveled from her temple down to her cheek and disappeared under her long black hair did nothing to detract from how attractive she was.

"What are you?" Brent asked, unable to take his eyes off of her.

She lifted her chin, defiantly. "Who are you? And where did you take my sister?"

"You were the only one we found in the cage. Was she running out there with you?"

"You know damn well she wasn't. You caught her last week. Where is she?" she snarled.

"Fuck!" Ty stated bluntly, finally understanding what their female was saying. "You wanted to get trapped because you're looking for your sister."

Her eyes darted around the room looking for a weapon in case she needed it. "Where did you take her?"

Brent growled at the thought that his mate had intentionally allowed herself to get captured. He wasn't very happy with the fact that their mate was under the impression that they were both a part of the poacher's crew.

"We were the ones who liberated you from the trapper's camp. I'm Brent and he's Ty. You're safe here. We aren't going to hurt you. Do you remember anything from before you were captured?"

"I'm Shiloh. My sister Shadoh and I are identical twins, well almost. We look the same except for our markings. Mine are on this side of my face and Shadoh's are on the opposite side. Our mother was Tibetan and our father was American. Our mother was born a full-blooded snow leopard shifter; both her parents were from an arranged marriage. When my grandmother Yeshe, found out our mother was in love with an American, she helped her to escape with him before my grandfather could give her hand in marriage to a man who was very well known for being unstable." Shiloh sat on the edge of the bed. "Shadoh is all the family I have left, I have to find her."

"As your mates, we will help," Ty abruptly announced.

Shiloh frowned, her heart sinking as she realized what the situation was. One of these men was her mate and one was to be Shadoh's.

"I... Um, I don't know how to say this without upsetting one of you." She stood and moved to stand in front of the one called Brent. She reached up on her tiptoes and inhaled a deep breath. She closed her eyes to concentrate and then exhaled slowly. She then moved to where Ty stood and repeated the process, only this time when she took in his scent, she began to purr and before she could stop her own reaction, her tongue peeked out and she licked up the side of his neck.

She took a step away from Ty and gently placed her hand on Brent's cheek. "I am sorry, but you are not my mate. You belong to Shadoh."

"Well fuck! I guess that's both good news and bad." He slapped Ty on the back, "Congrats man."

Ty placed himself between the bear and his mate. "Hey man, we'll find her. You're not alone. I know it's almost Christmas Eve, but if we can get a few hours' sleep, I say we head out first thing in the morning and start looking."

"You guys take the cabin. I'm gonna go and let Brent know what kind of fucked up situation I'm in and see if Lexi knows how to find the king dick of the poachers." Brent conceded, then walked out the door, locking it behind him.

Duke opened the fridge to inspect the contents. It was always the same. When the elder-women of the clan knew he and his brother were expected, they never failed to stock the fridge and freezer with food. Without a second thought, he began to mix up a batch of cinnamon pancakes. He sliced up some green apples and placed them on the stove to stew in some sugar syrup before pouring the batter into the pan. The knock at the door startled him, considering it was nearly midnight. He checked the pots and pans on the stove and ran to unlock the front door. Before looking to see who it was, he quickly returned to where he was preparing the feast in hopes of winning some brownie points with his mate.

Brent glanced around for Lexi, only to have Duke nod his head in the direction of the bathroom. Brent mouthed an 'Oh' and shrugged his shoulder, then sat down heavily in one of the kitchen chairs at the table.

"I thought I'd found my mate," Brent began. He paused only briefly as Lexi walked out of the bathroom dressed in a nightshirt that resembled one of his brother's t-shirts.

Duke waited for him to go on as he continued to cook. "So, what's changed?" he asked, confused.

"Shiloh, the snow leopard is my mate's identical twin. She's been trying to get herself captured so she could locate her sister. Apparently, a couple of weeks ago, Shadoh was taken while the two were out hunting." He cracked his knuckles in frustration. "Shiloh and the wolf belong together which means I need to know everything Lexi knows about the syndicate." His hands were shaking at the thought that he may miss out on his one chance to find and claim his happy ever after. If he lost her before he'd even found her and gotten to know her, he would forever possess a gaping void in his soul.

"Lexi, I know my brother is an idiot. I'm also aware that sometimes the filter between his head and his mouth doesn't work properly. But we only get one mate, and I can't bear to think of what life would be like without her in it. Will you help me find Shadoh?"

"I'd be happy to help, if I had a computer, with internet access. All my files are in the cloud. Maybe if we went over them together, we might find something that

I've overlooked or missed. Plus, now that I know about the whole shifter thing, I have a something new to work with."

Duke served up the pancakes and arranged everything neatly on the table. Setting a plate for all three of them, he returned with the ice-cream and sat down. He served up two for Lexi, then added the apple sauce and a side dollop of ice-cream.

"I hope you like them. I've been craving them," he explained, leaning close enough to compare Lexi's own natural scent to the aroma of the ingredients on her plate. He then set about helping himself and indicated that Brent was on his own to grab what he wanted. As Brent lifted his fork to his lips, he narrowed his eyes and stared at Duke. Duke gave an almost unnoticeable shake of his head, telling his brother to shut the fuck up. He knew his brother could also make the connection between the aroma of the food and Lexi's intoxicating scent. Brent shrugged his shoulder, glad that he'd chosen the maple syrup instead of the apple sauce, because that would just be wrong on so many levels.

Trying hard not to think about it, Brent focused his attention on how they were going to find his mate.

"So, Lexi, what kind of information do you have?" he asked.

"I have a list of areas where they've stopped. Maybe if we can match them to known shifter groups or packs, then we can identify those people who've been taken." She placed another forkful of heaven into her mouth, chewed then swallowed before asking, "Under normal circumstances, humans would report a missing person. What would you do if one of your kind disappeared?"

"It would depend on the age of the shifter. It isn't unheard of that a male will leave his clan in search of his mate if she isn't part of it," Duke offered, "Cubs rarely go missing, and are usually found within the first twenty-four hours. Most of the time it is because they've gotten lost after traveling too far from the pack and their tracks get covered by fresh snow. We try to teach them from an early age to rub against the trees to leave their scent on the bark. Unfortunately, though, boys will be boys."

"I guess it's safe to presume that the both of you know this from previous experience." Lexi looked at Brent then Duke.

"You could say that," Brent confessed, "I was the one always getting lost and Duke was the boy scout who saved my hide more than once."

He finished the last of his plate and stood. "I guess I'll go and get some sleep. We have an early start in the morning. We'll have to let the elders know. Duke," he paused, "can I have a word with Lexi... in private?"

Duke frowned and looked at Lexi then back at his brother. "You'd have to ask Lexi."

Before Brent could repeat his request, Lexi said, "Sure," as she studied Duke's features. "Duke was about to go and have a shower, weren't you?"

He gave her a lop-sided smile, which made her want to kiss the damn thing right off his face. Duke pushed back his chair, said good night to his brother and headed for the bathroom, just because his mate had told him to.

Brent waited until he could hear the sound of the water running before he spoke. He motioned for Lexi to move towards the front door, then he whispered, "Lexi, I know you don't know us, but we are family now. Duke can't scent the change in you, only because he's trying to damp down his bear's natural instincts. My circumstances are different; my bear is restless and very close to the surface at the moment and will be until I have my mate in my arms. He will love you like no other man ever can. I don't want to pressure you or scare you, but you heard what I said about only having one chance at finding our mate."

"I... I'm..." Lexi stumbled, not sure what she was supposed to say or how she felt. She wanted that family so desperately her bones ached.

"Lexi, you already smell like his bear. He's done more than imprint on you." Brent wasn't certain how much to say. Finally, he shared Lexi's secret which she herself didn't know she had. "The cub you carry will need its father. Duke's a good man." He kissed his fingertips and placed them on Lexi's belly. "He won't know unless you tell him, so in the meantime, don't put yourself in any unnecessary danger. If anything happens to you and he finds out you're carrying his cubs, he'll go nuts. Good night Lexi."

"Wait, what?" she asked, not certain if her perception was hindered by how tired she was or by what Brent had just said to her.

"The water just turned off, I have to go." He stepped outside, then added. "Yeah, we bears tend to come in twos." He saluted Lexi's stunned expression and headed for the underground cave he and his brother had discovered when they were kids. He removed his clothes and allowed his bear to take control. At first his bear seemed agitated and paced the mouth of the cave, but then he curled up into a boulder-size lump and fell asleep, knowing the first rays of the sun would wake him where he lay.

CHAPTER 9

Lexi blinked several times, trying to comprehend what Brent had just told her. She couldn't fathom why she was so drawn to Duke. It was beyond crazy. They'd known each other for only a couple of days, but her hands itched to touch him.

When he walked out from the bathroom in nothing but a towel, she stared. No, she openly gawked at the droplets that trickled down his body. She found herself wanting to growl when they all but evaporated from his skin by the time they'd reached his navel. Lexi blushed as she noticed Duke's cock becoming more solid and bulging behind the fluffy towel.

Duke could feel butterflies in the pit of his stomach as he stood stock still, not wanting to break the spell. He could feel his cock hardening as Lexi's eyes caressed his torso. His bear growled inside his head, but he held his breath and waited. When Lexi's cheeks became heated with colour, she lifted her appraisal up to his face immediately shifting her gaze to the fireplace.

"Don't stop," Duke pleaded.

Lexi bit her lower lip as if undecided on what she wanted to do. A second later, her gaze flashed back in his direction. Duke took one step closer, and at the same time, Lexi's feet shifted without her permission. With only an arm's length between them, Duke spoke softly, "Touch me?" he urged, needing the contact with his mate. "I accept you as my mate, Lexi Cavanagh. I welcome you into my life and I hope that one day you will see passed my faults and flaws and grant me the privilege to claim you as my mate and I, yours."

Lexi's hand cautiously rose and her fingertips traced the same path as the water droplets, which she'd studied intently only minutes ago. She licked her lips, eliciting a groan from Duke. His muscles twitched as though her touch was electrified. His breathing became short, sharp and shallow, as her fingers passed his navel and brushed the smitten of hair that led to his aching shaft. He clenched his fists to stop himself from reaching out.

Lexi breached the distance as another bead of water started its journey south. Only standing tall enough to reach it as it slid over his pec, her tongue poked out and abruptly ended its navigation irresistibly close to his puckered nipple. Duke began to pant as her lips sailed over and around it in a tentative action which resounded all the way down to his balls, making them heavy with desire. Still, he resisted moving. He wanted Lexi to know that he belonged to her. He just hoped and prayed she didn't stop whatever she was doing to him. He liked it as complicated as it was between them. He wanted this more than his next drawn breath.

"Fuck!" he cried, as her teeth grazed it. Momentarily distracted by her intentions, his fingers threaded through her hair to encourage her attentions. Lexi's hand met with the top of the towel and with a quick flick of her wrist it hit the floor. Her hands settled on his hips and she manoeuvred him the few paces towards the bed. She flattened both hands on his chest and she pushed firmly. Duke obeyed, falling backwards onto the mattress. Lexi leaned over and circled the base of his cock with one hand. Standing his shaft up straight, she licked the underside from the top of her hand to tip of his crown. Her tongue lapped several times at the eye of his penis, tasting his pre-cum. She revolved her tongue, whirling it around the crown, before pursing her lips to form a tight 'O' ring. The knob of his cock popped past the imitation entrance. She flattened her tongue to the floor of her mouth, then curled the tip to flick gently from side to side over the membrane strand under the mushroom head. Lexi allowed her saliva to lubricate her dissension as she inched his cock in deeper until it hit the back of her throat. Breathing through her nose, she swallowed, emulating the convulsing muscles of a pussy in the throes of an orgasm. Lexi continued to hold her breath on the downward glide to the back of her throat; swallow, breathe, swallow, and breathe. On the upward slide, she used the strength of her tongue to apply pressure to Duke's shaft, driving his pleasure higher as his bulbous crown met the firmness of the roof of her mouth. This was one act she knew she was superior at and it fed her own desire by fuelling the limits of her control. Several rounds and Duke's hands were fisting the bed covers, and he was groaning loudly, immersed in the immense pleasure his mate was awarding him.

"Baby, your mouth is pure sin. I'm gonna cum if you don't stop," he gasped.

"Mmmhmm," Lexi hummed in acknowledgment. The added vibrations, along with her mouth's expert forgery of fucking a warm wet pussy, was enough to propel him over the edge. Surge after surge of liquid heat shot forth from Duke's pulsing cock as he growled. "Fuuuuuuck!"

Lexi quickly swallowed with every pulse, increasing the sensation by mimicking a mutual orgasm, drawing out the mind-blowing ambiance until every tensed muscle in Duke's body collapsed boneless to the bed.

"I think you just killed me," he accused, jokingly. "I'd pinch myself to see if I'm dreaming, but I don't think I can move." He chuckled, then complained "Ouch!" when Lexi pinched him.

"Nope. Definitely still alive and breathing, Mr. Greyson." She was about to crawl onto the bed when Duke shook his head from side to side.

"Take it off for me baby," he asked gently.

Lexi reached for the hem of the shirt she was wearing and slowly lifted it up and over her head, dropping it on the floor beside the bed. Duke smiled. "Lexi, you have no idea what you do to me. You're beautiful and I would honestly do anything to make you my mate." Lexi's eyes settled on his already swelling cock. She wondered if the fast return to sexual readiness had something to do with his shifter side. Lexi placed her knee on the bed and climbed up to straddle Duke's hips, opening her already wet centre to slide along his rapidly hardening shaft. In a reverse cowgirl position, she placed her hand on Duke's knee and rose up. With her free hand, she lifted his cock to rest at her entrance, then with both hands just above the bend of his knees, she rolled her hips.

Her body stretched inch by inch as she worked him inside her aching snatch until her lower lips kissed the base of his cock. She felt the inner walls of her pussy twitch twice from the exquisite pleasure of being filled to the hilt. Lexi closed her eyes and savoured the sensation. Using the position of her hands, she anchored them on Duke's knees, then leaned forward and began an exquisitely slow ride. Her openly splayed lower lips allowed her clit to brush against the base of Duke's rock-hard rod with every downward impalement.

Duke felt the ultimate trust Lexi was affording him by turning her back to him. It was the most entrancing thing he'd ever seen, the way her rounded cheeks rose to play peekaboo with his cock as it found the perfect hiding place. He loved watching himself slide in and out of Lexi's body. It was as though she were branding him as hers. Finally, unable to stay still any longer, he began to pump his hips up to meet her every downward movement, thrusting into her harder and harder as they both began to fill the air with sounds of pleasure.

Duke sat up with his chest to Lexi's back and kissed the base of her neck. Instinctively she tilted her head to give him access.

"Are you sure?" Duke asked not wanting to take what wasn't freely given or to misinterpret the gesture.

"Do it," Lexi cried out, close to completion.

Duke slid one arm around Lexi's front

to cup her breast and to pinch her pebbled nipple. The other slid down to her swollen clit which he circled it with his fingertips. Lexi whimpered in desperation and as Duke's bite struck hard and fast at her shoulder, her body exploded into a million fragments. The blood rushing in her ears muffled the words he spoke, but she was pretty certain they were some kind of ritual. As her body went limp in his lap, her pussy still grasped to hold onto its mate's connection, he moved them carefully onto the bed where she fell asleep in his arms.

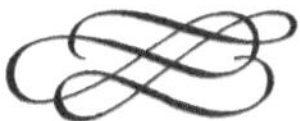

Brent woke well before the sun broke on the horizon. He quickly shifted and got dressed. He was eager to find and save his mate from whatever hell she was in at the moment. He had dreamt of the perfect Christmas and now he wanted it more than anything.

Both Duke and Lexi felt as though they'd had next to no sleep; which technically was true to some degree. When they heard Brent knock on the door to indicate it was time to make a move, they quickly dressed and were out the door as fast as they could.

The wolf opened the door before Brent

could knock. "We're ready when you are." Ty and Shiloh had spent the night getting to know one another on a mental level. He'd explained to Shiloh that there was no rush now that they'd found each other, they could take things one step at a time. Although they had both struggled and lost against the need to touch their mate, it had gone no further than cuddling and holding hands at this stage. Ty wanted to know that his mate's twin was safe and with her mate before he burdened her with all the things that were involved with being the mate of a wolf. Her safety and her happiness were the most important things to him, and at the moment, that was connected to finding her missing twin Shadoh.

Ty spoke to Brent, "I'm wondering if any of the poacher's vehicles had navigational trackers on board. If they did, we may be able to figure out where they've been traveling to and from."

Lexi and Duke joined the conversation and were introduced to Shiloh by her mate Ty.

"We need a map so we can triangulate their movements and correlate that with the known clans and packs in those areas. If there are others missing, we may be able to get more help along the way," Lexi offered.

They all hiked together towards the stranded vehicles at the edge of the parks boundary. They found the keys in the ignition of both vehicles and decided to break into two groups. Duke and Lexi in one vehicle while the others jumped into the second. Duke started the engine while Lexi accessed the GPS and began flicking through the destinations. There was one that showed up several times and she leapt out to see if the other team had discovered the same information.

"Yeah, it's a good place to start," Brent said hopeful. "We might get lucky. At least it isn't that far from here, probably only a two-and-a-half-hour drive."

Lexi didn't even hear Duke as he came up from behind her until he spoke, "Let's head there first."

~

The trip was made in relative silence. Lexi was nervous about putting herself in danger. If Brent was right, and she was pregnant, she didn't want to put her life or the life of her unborn at risk. At the same time, she didn't want Duke to be distracted by her condition either, possibly putting himself in danger as a result. In the end, she opted to save the news for a better delivery time.

They arrived at an isolated property with a large house built not far from the road. Parking on the side of the road, Duke put the windows down and closed his eyes. Lexi watched as Ty and Brent appeared to do the same in the vehicle in front.

Both Ty and Brent leapt from their SUV and walked towards them. Duke opened his door to get out.

"I can scent several different species," Ty conceded. "I don't know about you guys but I'm thinking we should leave the ladies here and shift to get closer."

"I'm not staying here, not when my sister is inside." Shiloh, suddenly spoke from beside the men. "I'm going in too."

"I'm going as well," Lexi spoke up from the passenger seat.

"Lexi, I'd rather you didn't, you can't shift," Duke's concern noticeable in his tone.

"Maybe not, but I can drive and I can shoot," Lexi responded with conviction. "This is one of the vehicles that is unknown to the owner, so I can pretty much drive straight up to the house without drawing too much attention to myself. I'm not sure if you noticed, but there's enough ammo and weapons in the backseat to fend off a small army."

They split up; Ty and Shiloh headed in from the rear, Brent and Duke changed into their bears and took the side, while Lexi drove straight up the driveway.

As they drew nearer, Shiloh became nervous and started making strange noises. "Are you alright?" Ty asked.

"I don't know why, but something feels wrong about all of this. It almost feels like a trap." The words had no sooner left her mouth than the echo of a discharged weapon resounded around them. "Claim me," she cried as she staggered.

Ty did as his mate commanded, quickly sinking his canines into the flesh at Shiloh's collar before he to felt the bite of a dart and they collapsed on the ground together.

"You stubborn little bitch!" Harraki swore. "I should kill you both now," he snarled, standing over the couple.

Lexi slammed on the brakes and took aim at the male standing over Ty and his mate. "You so much as move a muscle asshole and I'll put a bullet in your brain."

Harraki lifted his nose to the air, then sneered, "You do that little human, and my guards will tear you to pieces."

"Fine, you leave me no choice." Lexi discharged her 9mm blowing out the bastard's kneecap. As he crashed to the ground, she pulled out a zip tie and cuffed his hands together behind his back.

"You're not dead, yet." Lexi had no doubts this was one of the kingpins involved in the capture of shifters and the slaughter of harmless wildlife.

On hearing the commotion, Duke and Brent made their way to where the action seemed to be happening. Pride burst within Duke's chest when he discovered the spirits had sent him a fierce female. She may not be a bear, but she sure as hell exhibited the courage of one.

"Duke, you have to stay with these guys. We can't leave them exposed." Lexi took charge. "Brent, you come with me," she commanded, pulling a set of keys from the pocket of the man she'd shot.

She raced back to the SUV and shoved a few clips into her pockets, then made her way along the side of the house towards the front door. Brent trailed her to protect her back. Once at the entrance, Lexi tried the knob only to find it locked. She quickly shuffled through the keys looking for one that fitted the lock. The first one didn't work. As she slid the second one into place, the door flew open and a man in black released his hold on a wolf. He leapt at Lexi only to be knocked to the ground by Brent as he interceded the attack.

"Fuck you!" Lexi yelled, shooting the man in the shoulder as he raised a weapon in Brent's direction.

Strangely, the second the wolf realized they were not the enemy. He whimpered and lay down on his belly, bowing his head. Lexi frowned and looked at Brent for his reaction. The wolf surged past Lexi and latched onto the neck of the man in black, his teeth rendering a death grip. Lexi gasped when she saw the gun in his hand drop to the floor and his life expired before he could fire the shot that was aimed at her.

Lexi and Brent moved quickly inside the premises, checking rooms as they proceeded. The wolf they'd left behind ran past them, stopped and looked at them before taking off down a long corridor. Lexi glanced at Brent, then followed, knowing that it was possible that there were other men waiting in ambush. At the end of the hall, the wolf scratched at a door. With her weapon raised, Lexi swung the door open.

The wolf took off like a hellhound on a mission, but she and Brent entered with caution. They discovered several cells with a variety of wild cats, wolves and bears inside them.

"Are they all shifters?" she asked Brent, who growled and gave a single nod of his head. "Fuck! Do you see your mate?"

Lexi studied each of the caged animals. "Why do they all have collars on?" she said more to herself than to anyone in particular.

"That, my dear, is to prevent them from changing." replied a man wearing a white coat.

"Who the fuck are you?" Lexi asked pointing her weapon at the man who resembled a doctor or a scientist. She suddenly felt ill with the thought that these amazing species were being experimented on.

His hands rose beside his head, palms facing her, "I am no threat to you. I want what they all want. Freedom, although mine comes at a heavy price. Harraki has my mate. I haven't seen her in over a year.

You will need his fingerprint to release the locks on the collars."

"What exactly is he doing here? What's the point of all this?" Lexi demanded. She wanted answers, and she wanted to know this was as far as it went, but something in her gut told her there was much more to this little enterprise.

"Harraki is the man who runs the Northern Auction House of highly sought-after procurements and acquisitions. Liberating this compound won't even make a dent in his operation…"

Brent shifted, his hand clasping around the man's throat above the collar, "Where's the snow leopard?"

His eyebrows lifted. "Please," he begged, "if you kill me, you will also be killing my mate."

Brent released his hold. "Then you better tell me where I can find my mate."

"She was brought in around five days ago. She didn't take to being drugged very well, so she has been kept in a different area. Harraki told me that she was too valuable for him to lose. I run regular health checks on everyone. They all understand that I can't shift, the same as they can't. I'm Doctor Graham Harris. If you follow me, I'll take you to the infirmary."

"Lexi, can you see if any of other keys will open the doors on these cells?"

"On it," she stated, moving to the closest one. "Okay cougar, just so we're clear, I am not food." She slid the key into the lock, and cried out, "Booyah!" when it turned and the cage was unlocked. Lexi soon discovered that each of the cells used the same key and before long, she had her own army of wildlife surrounding her.

"Come on guys and gals, this way. Let's go find a thumb to unlock these collars." As she reached the front door, she felt the need to advise the group of shifters, "I know your first instinct will be to kill this asshole, but we need all the information we can get from him. If there's others out there like you, we have to try to save them as well. I think it's about time the hunters became the hunted." The mutual response was howls, growls and snarls as they walked to where Duke was standing guard over Harraki.

"Which one of your thumbs unlocks the collars?" Lexi growled in disgust at Harraki. He smirked and shook his head, refusing to give her the information she was asking for. "Fine, you leave me no choice than to take them both off." She smiled back, pulling a dagger from a thigh hostler.

"Wait," Harraki, yelled. "It's my right one."

"Either you're a coward or you're just very stupid. If so much as one thing goes wrong and one of them gets hurt, I will personally cut out your heart and feed it to my mate. I hate cruelty to animals."

"I am the last full-blooded snow leopard shifter from Tibet," Harraki informed her.

"Good, then you can answer to your fellow shifters instead of me. Now shut the fuck up and stop stalling. Is it your right thumb or your left?"

Self-preservation must have suddenly kicked in and Harraki answered, "Left, but if you untie my hands, I will unlock the collars for you."

"Not a chance in hell," Lexi answered. She grabbed the thumb on his left hand and twisted it to dislocate the joint at the same time the blade met with his flesh. Holding up Harraki's thumb, Lexi called out, "Who's first?" The shifters all lined up, and one by one, Lexi unlocked their collars. Finally, Brent walked out of the house wearing the Doctor's white coat, carrying Shadoh in his arms. "Doctor, would you be kind enough to give me your collar?"

The Doctor leaned down and allowed Lexi to unlock the band around his neck. "Thanks," she smiled, before turning back to Harraki.

"For the trouble you have caused to myself and these beautiful creatures this Christmas, I hereby sentence you to this form until the day you die." She fixed the Doctor's discarded collar around Harraki's neck before turning to the group of shifters still in their animal form and clearly announced, "Bon appetite."

~

The rest of Christmas Eve was spent making certain that people were returned to their homes. The only one they couldn't immediately help was the Doctor. He'd chosen to stay at the house to watch over Harraki in his prison cell until the male revealed the whereabouts of his beloved mate. Lexi and the Doctor had exchanged contact information and after the New Year, they would work together to find the remainder of the missing shifters.

They all sat around the fire, Ty and Shiloh, beside Brent and his mate Shadoh, Lexi and Duke. The elders reminded them that this was probably only the beginning for all of them. As midnight struck, they raised their cups of hot chocolate and welcomed in Christmas together.

Duke turned his head to whisper in Lexi's ear, "The spirits have sent me the perfect mate, although I will have to admit you did scare me a little back there today."

Lexi giggled, "Okay, I suppose it's safe to say I may have been a little overbearing but you can blame that on my maternal instincts to protect what's mine. I guess now is as good a time as any to give you your Christmas present although it may take a while for you to unwrap it. It's coming via special delivery." She placed Duke's hand on her belly and watched his face as his initial stunned look melted into one of pride and glee.

"We certainly have a few things to celebrate." He kissed her gently, then held out his hand as he stood and announced. "Lexi and I are calling it a night. We wish you a very Merry Christmas and to all a good night."

ABOUT THE AUTHOR

Melissa Bell lives in Brisbane, Australia. She has loved to read since the age of twelve when she discovered 'To Kill A Mocking Bird', previous to reading this book she hated reading. With a couple of handfuls of years and thousands of books later she wanted to try writing.

When she is writing, she loves to listen to her favorite Australian bands - Birds of Tokyo and Karnivool.

She most recently made the USA Today Best Sellers List in October 2021 and has now set her sights on reaching the NY Times Best Sellers List.

She enjoys good food and good company when she's not trying to concentrate on what she's writing. She loves to laugh as laughter makes the world go round not money. Unfortunately laughter doesn't pay the bills unless you're a really well-known stand-up comedian. Which she is not. She is hoping that this is the start of an exciting adventure as a published Author, and that maybe something amazing will come of it. She would like to invite you all to join her on her journey.

Please keep an eye out for other books by Melissa Bell.

Dutiful Gods Series

Book #1 Destiny's Fate

Book #2 Taming Destruction

Book #3 Morpheus's Dream

Book #4 Defying Death

Five Brothers Series

Book#1 Houston

Book#2 Felan

Book#3 Tate

Book #4 Channon

Book #4.5 Lupe

Book #5 London

Brody and Blaez will be next in this series -
TBA

www.ingramcontent.com/pod-product-compliance
Lightning Source LLC
Chambersburg PA
CBHW031426150726
47989CB00002B/817